BEAR·SLEEP·SOUP

Story and Pictures by Jasper Tomkins

GREEN TIGER PRESS

Published by Simon & Schuster
New York · London · Toronto · Sydney · Tokyo · Singapore

GREEN TIGER PRESS
Simon & Schuster Building, Rockefeller Center
1230 Avenue of the Americas, New York, New York 10020
Copyright © 1989 by Jasper Tomkins
All rights reserved including the right of reproduction
in whole or in part in any form.
GREEN TIGER PRESS is an imprint of Simon & Schuster.
Manufactured in Hong Kong

10   9   8   7   6   5

ISBN: 0-671-75278-2

For Pup the Night Good,
Princess of Horizonshine

Dear Bears,
My offer still stands. You are welcome here any time.
Remember, you don't have to swim to the island. Just
send a postcard and I'll send you a ferry ticket.

One crisp fall day the bears collected everything they needed for a very special soup. All afternoon they took turns stirring the steaming pot. Of course, baby bear spent most of the time sleeping.

Finally, it was agreed that the soup smelled
just right. When the bowls were all full,
the bears shouted out "Happy Sleeping"
to each other and began to slurp.

But while they were licking out their bowls, baby bear quietly emptied hers into a bush. She did not like the soup. In fact, she thought it smelled terrible.

Next, it was time to wash the dishes. The bears looked very serious and did not say a word. So baby bear carefully dried her bowl and did not make a sound.

When the dishes were neatly put away,
the bears sat beside the fire and each
did ten sit-ups. Then they stood on their
tip-toes and tried to touch the stars. Baby
bear thought it was all very silly, but she
stretched as high as she could anyway.

The bears all began to yawn. Baby bear was ready to dance, but she pretended to yawn just like the rest of her family.

"Last bear to bed puts the fire out,"
mumbled mama bear as she stumbled
toward the cave with sleepy eyes.

Baby bear was trying very hard not to laugh, but the bears were all so funny. They were stumbling and tumbling, trying to hold each other up as they went into the cave.

She watched with a smile as they flopped
into a pile. Then they began to snore.
Baby bear laughed. She had never
seen her whole family asleep at once.
She thought they must be playing.

She poked and she prodded and she
twisted some ears. But no one moved.
"Now wake up!" she shouted in her
biggest voice. "It's a beautiful night for
a swim." But her family was far away
in the land of dreams.

Baby bear walked away from the great furry pile and did a wild dance around the fire. She had never done that before.

She danced over to the shelf of clean dishes and balanced her bowl right on the tip of her nose. She had always wanted to do that.

She sang a song to the moon and watched the clouds go across its face. She had never sung the song before.

Baby bear wondered what her friends were doing. She walked down to the river but the fish were all asleep. She had never been up so late before.

In the forest all was quiet. The mice were asleep. The squirrels were asleep, and the birds had their heads under their wings. She had never seen that before.

Baby bear listened to the wind whispering through the trees. Then the wolves began to howl. She had never heard that before.

She ran as fast as she could, back to the dying fire. She climbed up the side of the great warm soup pot and jumped right in. Fortunately, the bears had been too tired to wash it out.

Baby bear licked and she scraped and she licked until that pot was cleaner than it had been in a very long time.

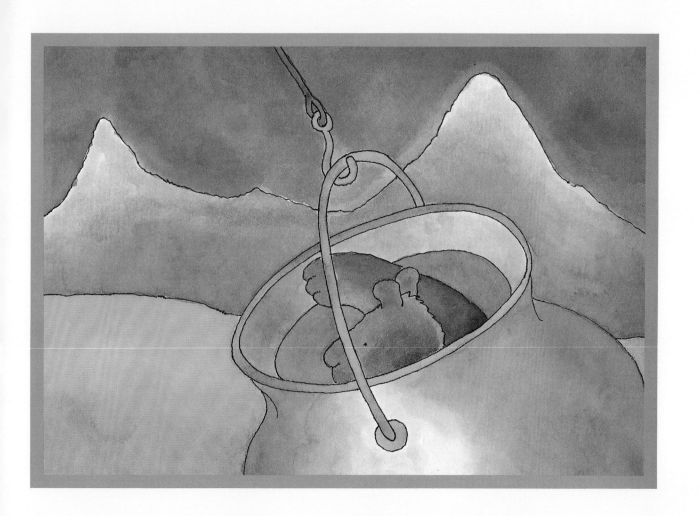

She tried to crawl out, but she was so tired she slid back into the pot and fell asleep right then and there. She would have slept there the whole winter but the wolves began to howl once again.

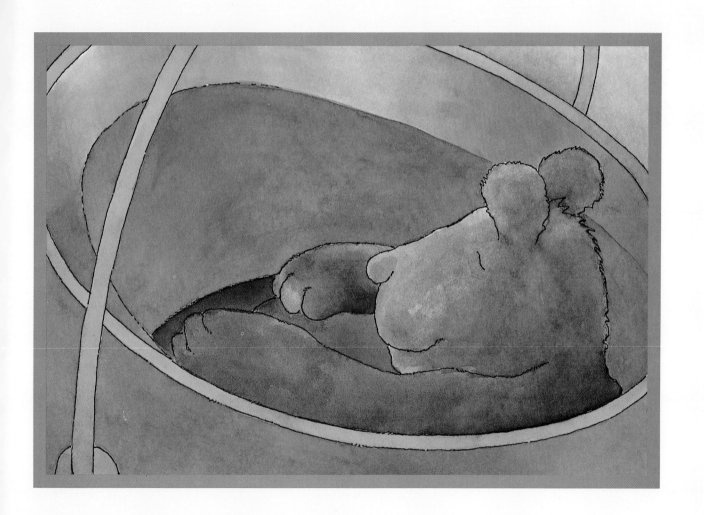

Baby bear was out of the soup pot and swinging on the fire bucket rope before she even knew she was awake again.

As a cloud of steam hissed up past the moon, baby bear stumbled towards the cave.

She fell and she rolled and she finally just crawled the rest of the way. Slowly, slowly, with her eyes barely open she dragged herself toward her sleeping family. It was just beginning to snow.

She crawled right up the side of the great pile of sleepy, warm arms and legs. And up on the top was the softest of furry nests. It was just the right size for a small baby bear who was already sound asleep.

The wolves howled and they laughed. The ice crackled, the stars snapped, the blizzards roared, and the wind whipped around the trees. But baby bear slept through it all.

She had dreams of warm places by rivers full of fish. Buckets of berries were under every tree.

She slept and she slept. Baby bear did not wake up until she heard the first flower quietly push its way up through the snow in the spring.